T0194114

ALTERMAN BIG CLUB

Bridge System

SCORING WITH MASTER POINTS AND THE
OPPOSITE SEX........AND IT'S EASY AS ABC

By Dr. Stanley B. Alterman

iUniverse, Inc.
Bloomington

ALTERMAN BIG CLUB
Bridge System

iUniverse books may be ordered through booksellers or by contacting:

iUniverse
1663 Liberty Drive
Bloomington, IN 47403
www.iuniverse.com
1-800-Authors (1-800-288-4677)

Because of the dynamic nature of the Internet, any web addresses or links contained in this book may have changed since publication and may no longer be valid. The views expressed in this work are solely those of the author and do not necessarily reflect the views of the publisher, and the publisher hereby disclaims any responsibility for them.

Any people depicted in stock imagery provided by Thinkstock are models, and such images are being used for illustrative purposes only.

Certain stock imagery © Thinkstock.

ISBN: 978-1-4759-7755-4 (sc)
ISBN: 978-1-4759-7753-0 (e)

Library of Congress Control Number: 2013903316

Printed in the United States of America

iUniverse rev. date: 3/19/2013

TABLE OF CONTENTS

FORWARD

Think about it: Big club for strong hands; weak no trump for balanced hands; therefore, other opening bids are unbalanced and limited in high card points. No other system is as easy to learn. It's as easy to learn as ABC. Eliminating system mistakes will dramatically improve your results. Winning is always more fun! Furthermore, I'm often asked what is the best system or conventions to play. I invariably answer, "The same ones your partner plays." Invest a little time with your partner to learn the Alterman Big Club. It is as easy to learn as ABC. Eliminating systemic mistakes will dramatically improve your results. Furthermore, Dr. Alterman has personally guaranteed that all of your finesses will win (only if you peek, of course) or double your money back.

Lew Finkel (3 time world senior silver medalist)

ACKNOWLEDGEMENT

Much appreciation to Donald Schlenger and Robert Goodman and the others that learned the Alterman Big Club and gave me continuous, valuable recommendations

1. INTRODUCTION

You all have purchased many Bridge Books and found most of them impossible to use effectively. The most useful thing I did with one of them is when I killed an irritating fly at the Philadelphia Bridge National Championship last year. Why is this bridge book different from all other bridge books in the rest of the world? This sounds like the start of the Seder on Passover!

First because we will Pass Over (get it?......Matzo, Jews, Sand, Moses, Red Sea.....you know) all the bridge hand examples and little tests and try to educate you to learn an easy, effective bridge bidding system by yourself or with a willing, loving partner. Passover celebrates when the Jews were led out of Egypt by Moses. 5000 years ago the Jews didn't play bridge, eat Chinese food or have nose jobs for that matter. They didn't even have a bridge. If they did, Moses wouldn't have asked for God's help to part the Red Sea; they would just have built a bridge and shortened the entire biblical story. I know those are different bridges! The Alterman Big Club will try to build a bridge from bridge to sex and fun. What Moses had was lots of people; all Jews, much like many bridge clubs in Palm Beach County. Not all South Florida bridge players are Jews, except in Palm Beach many are. In spite of the concentrated number of Jews, it's pretty safe to play bridge in Palm Beach. Somehow you don't see a large number of terrorists playing bridge. I wonder why? Maybe it's the need for some terrorists to pray so often which would interrupt four hour bridge tournaments and long boring bridge lessons. Maybe it's difficult and uncomfortable sitting so long at bridge tables with bombs strapped to your waist. Who knows? So we are dealing with a safe, sexy subject, bridge. Even though safe from terrorists, bridge and love for that matter are dangerous battlefields containing mines, IEDs and other booby traps. The author has navigated these war zones for the last half century providing innovative military solutions in Electronic Warfare, Stealth, Information Operations to Cyber and Counter-Cyber security. He has taken this unique expertise and blended successful KISS (Keep It Simple Stupid) principles from the defence industry to bridge and social networking to sex. As his old cold war adversary, Adm. Gorshkov of the Soviet Union Navy often said, "Better is the enemy of good enough". Stan puts this important concept to work in bridge and love as effectively as he turned it against the now defunct Soviet Union. Seduce your adversary into your "Fog of War" and avoid his attempts at the same thing to you.

The bridge techniques developed by the author over the last five years have been demonstrated in Club, Country Club, regional and national events and vetted with a large variety of bridge masters. The concept of The Big Club was further tested by teaching a small group of Admirals Cove bridge players the ABC system and successfully competing in a high quality Interclub League team of eight IMP competition with season wins four of five years and one playoff second place. The system works!

You will take the core principles presented in The Alterman Big Club and build your own system or just play it as presented for more fun, master points and hopefully encounters with the opposite sex, or the same sex if that turns you on. To quote active long term bridge and sex player Mae West, "Good sex is like good bridge, if you don't have a good partner, you'd better have a good hand." The corollary to Mae West's wisdom is that "If your hand is so good that you don't care about your partner, the result won't be very interesting." Mae proved that you can still play bridge into your eighties and beyond and have good sex without your children gasping in horror when they find out that seniors have and talk about orgasms. I was going to call this book "52 Cards of Play", trying to ride the successful sex wave of "50 Shades of Grey" but my publisher, a lovely lady with a cute giggle, married, and probably very sexy, told me she preferred my "Big Club" title.......and imagine that, we have never even met. Maybe she talked to my girlfriend? I cannot pass up "50 Shades of Grey" and the next two books in this steaming trilogy without my learned technical analysis. (I am a Doctor and qualified to discuss this subject.....OK a Doctor of

So I'm Not a Professional Doctor....Don't Amateurs Count?

Bridge & Sex ...... Both Need Good Partner or Good Hand.

Engineering). No, I'm not off the bridge track. "50 Shades of Grey" has 20 Million readers and that number is exponentially growing. These readers are mostly women and the quantity of readers is about the same as the number of bridge players in the USA. There are 175,000 USA tournament players and at least 12 Million social players in this country and 5 to 10 times that many around the world or over 100 Million bridge geeks. The readers of "50 shades of Grey" are generally smart, successful, strong woman who fanaticise about male dominance in a modern woman's lib world where they have proudly turned men into wimps. Now they wonder what they are missing. The "Big Club" has a similar audience potential. Bright woman and men, successful, many living alone that fantasize what it would be like in bed with other bridge players who on the outside seem like a bunch of nerds but inside.....who knows?

Second, you will learn to love The Big Club and pass it on virally to everyone you know or meet to spread the gospel (a little religion in bridge is OK since prayer is a big part of the game). Unlike sex, bridge has no communicable diseases limiting the drive to get better and better by playing with anyone, even total strangers. In addition, the Ten Commandments has nothing negative to say about bridge. Maybe we can contribute just a bit to saving the world's great game that is currently dying because it doesn't connect with the young and young at heart. Ask Bill Gates who is throwing millions at the game to stem the tide. Along with his dear friend, Warren Buffett, both avid bridge players and two of the most successful businessmen of our time, they learned that bridge is the great equalizer and one of the great things in their lives. Buffett claims that playing bridge is so intense that a naked girl passing by might not attract his attention. That could be his age and the need for Viagra but bridge players can vouch for the intensity and excitement of the game. Once you know the basics of the game, bridge is very straightforward yet unbelievably complex; so complex that computers have not been able to master the bridge master and is one of the last games where the computer loses regularly. ABC may change that picture by introducing KISS principle bidding. Even though embraced by two of the worlds' wealthiest men, bridge is losing ground to TV, video games and instant gratification communications. Today, a casual invitation to a partner to join you for a "rubber" is more likely to be interpreted as a romp in the sack than an innocent game of cards. ABC eliminates the need for

Women love Bridge Players that use a strong Club with Precision.

I Said Let's play Alterman Big Club, not with it.

many complex bids necessary to make up for limitations of standard conventions in use today. Some people are so busy learning the various conventions and gadgets of the game; they never fully enjoy the game. People shouldn't be allowed to use conventions they don't understand. It's not fair to the opponents or their partners. Partners are extremely important. Who else are you to blame when you lose?

My housekeeper overheard the following at our home couples bridge game and ran out of my house screaming.

"Lay down and let's see what you've got." my friend said, "I've got strength, but no length."

His partner answered, "You jumped me twice when you didn't have the strength for one raise."

The other woman at the table was talking about protecting her honor and both gals at the table said, "Now it's time for a change and me to play with your guy and you can play with mine."

As my ex housekeeper quickly left, she could hear "Well, I guess we'll go home now. This is the last rubber."

Third, you will stand out in the crowd of bridge mediocrity and raise your game and love life to higher levels of satisfaction. Where else can you translate a Scissors Coup or a Reverse Squeeze in a bridge match to exciting positions in a lovers tryst. You don't need many finesses for success but squeezes are a great tool in your repertoire(s).

Forth, and most important, have a few laughs in the process if stimulating your bridge intellect.

Finally, the best advice I have ever given while teaching The Alterman Big Club is to relax a bit. Take deep breaths. Don't jump your partner so quickly. Concentrate on what is bid and what isn't. Bridge is like making love. Don't rush. Be Gentle. Get the feel of it. Enjoy it. Don't fight it. If you have what your partner wants and needs, you can score well in more ways than earning International Match Points. Let your Big Club work for you!

Bridge is like sex. Slow and easy better than jumping your partner.

Never Too Old for a Big Club

2. WHY DO PEOPLE PLAY BRIDGE?
... EXCITEMENT, RECOGNITION, MONEY AND SEX

There is a fine line between wanting to play bridge every day and mental illness. Bridge is the greatest card game in the world and one of the few that you don't have to play for money to enjoy (even so bridge can be and is one of the highest stakes money games to the real gambler/expert). Bridge is a game that simulates life and love making publically. It's a partnership game where communications is at its core and when successful can raise the excitement level of you and your partner simultaneously to a crescendo of orgasmic proportions. (oops! This book is for teenagers too). Although not legal, bridge communications often goes beyond the bidding box to eyes, body motions, beads of sweat, hand and other body language (much like dating). Even though it's competitive, bridge can bring people together, certainly at the bridge table, but often in bed at tournaments (I mean after, of course). It's a fun game played by people that want to have fun but often hide that fact with a very serious face and demeanour. Bridge is interesting since you will never (statistically that is) have the same hand twice (unless you forget to re deal the cards from the last game). Bridge, like good love making, takes time, effort and energy and is definitely good for your mind, body and soul. The Alterman Big Club will lead you into a new world of bridge that will enhance all the current aspects of the game that you now enjoy. You might even become a Big Club teacher and make a few bucks spreading the ABC virtues while keeping some lonely players happy at the card table, dinner table or even in bed. The top tournament players can make $10,000 to $15,000 each or more for playing in a championship like the Vanderbilt, plus expenses and a large bonus by sponsors, depending on performance and just winning at playing rubber bridge, a top player can make $250,000+ a year. The most well known big stakes rubber bridge game is the old "50-cent game," at the Regency Whist Club. That's about as big as bridge games get - 50 cents a point for each player (inflation may have doubled or tripled those stakes recently). A game contract that takes no more than 5 or 10 minutes is worth at least $250 to each player, and a grand slam at least $750. At that rate, it's easy to win, or lose, $5,000 or more in an afternoon.

I would be remiss at this point of not mentioning who the best of the best bridge players are today. Over the past 25 years a Texan named Robert Hamman has compiled the best record in the pressure-filled world of international tournament bridge with his longtime partner and fellow Texan, Bobby Wolff (Wolffie) a close second. Both were members of the six-player United States team that have been spectacular in the world championship Bermuda Bowl tournaments. Today, Italy's Claudio Nunes climbed to second place in the WBF Ranking. Fulvio Fantoni's, Nunes' partner, keeps the top position. Giorgio Duboin, another Italian player, is third at this moment. Bob Hamman (USA), the former number one of this list, is now fourth.

Hamman's position as the leader of the WBF Grand Master ranking (based on total placing points) remains unquestioned. The legendary Benito Garozzo (Italy/USA) is second here. Hammon and Wolffie regularly played at the Whist Club, probably adding to their sizeable income, with well know wealthy players like Alan (Ace) Greenberg, ex chairman of Bear, Stearns & Company, the brokerage firm, an avid bridge player. Added to that high stakes gambling group were the late Milton Petrie, who owned the big chain of women's clothing stores [the Petrie Stores Corporation], Jack Dreyfus, the founder of the Dreyfus mutual funds and the late Larry Tisch, the head of CBS and Loews.' The pleasure that these intensely competitive men, whose fortunes probably totaled in the multi billions, derive from trying to beat Hamman, or one of the other experts, is far greater than doing it to one another and well worth whatever "small change" it might cost them. Hamman insists that they were all strong players, but he must have felt like a kid who had found the keys to the candy store, his hand in the cookie jar or his finger in............OOPs! Censored.

Bridge is the greatest competitive game there is with tremendous depth. No matter how well you play you can always play better. In games such as poker there is an element of bluff and psychological pressure added but if the level of skill is at all close, the guy with the biggest bankroll has an enormous advantage. No one can totally dominate bridge, since even the best players, like Hammon win only 25% of the events they play in. In 1968, he joined the Aces, an all-star team of six players that had been organized a year or so earlier by Ira Corn, a Dallas conglomerateur. His goal was to regain supremacy for the United States from the famous Blue Team of Italy, which had dominated international bridge for more than a decade. They won the Bermuda Bowl for the United States in 1970 and 1971. (The bowl is now held in odd-numbered years, alternating with the Bridge Olympiad, one of four annual major championships run by the World Bridge Federation.) Wolff, who was one of the original Aces, was a member of the team, but he and Hamman didn't become partners until 1972, starting a very long, successful bridge career. Hamman and Wolff often played in the Vanderbilt Cup competition. It is the oldest and most prestigious of American bridge championships, having been established in 1929 by Harold Sterling Vanderbilt, great-grandson of the Commodore, America's Cup yachtsman and, beyond all that, the inventor, four years earlier, of the game of contract bridge.

Although it is of little practical importance, bridge still maintains the distinction between amateur and professional. Wolff and Hamman, like most of the star players, are registered professionals, but national and world tournaments are, in effect, open events. Teams of at least four players, and more often six - can be amateur, professional or mixed. Professionals play and are paid at local bridge clubs as well as big competitive master point tournaments. For a local game, inexperienced, lonely women often pay $150 or more for a professional to play with them to teach them the game, help them collect master points awarded to winners and possibly other extracurricular games and activities. These fees go up considerably for 7 day tournaments. Not a bad business! Play bridge! Vacation! Good food and drink! Then hop in the sack with some gal that wants to jump overcall your body as opposed to your bridge bid. The hidden secret of bridge is now exposed.

The key to bridge success, like penetrating the military fog of war and being successful in the blind emotions of love is spreading a cloud over the bridge battlefield and being able to see through the opponent's attempts to fog your vision. These experts keep their style of bidding and play relatively simple, but introduce complications that are meant to render opponents' procedures ineffective. We will discuss those important principles later in ABC.

Hamman says, "The most important thing is that it's not how good you are at your best, but how bad you are at your worst. Everyone is going to make horrendous errors from time to time, but experts are able to handle adversity better than most." Same is true for making love!

Best of all, bridge is a game that brings people together with common interests and basic skills as well as normal sexual appetites. I think that the best way to start on our road to success in bridge and the bedroom is to understand why some players win and some lose. 75% of bridge success is the communications (bidding) system that good partners use.

A lot goes to skills and concentration, which I can only help a little by trying to relax you about bridge. Some winning techniques "ain't" kosher as I described in my last best seller book (just kidding) on bridge, "One Peak is Worth Two Finesses". Peaking and cheating are not unheard of in the game of bridge, even at the highest levels. Between 1958 and 1975 allegations were so strong that the Italians were cheating that protective devices were introduced. For the first time in a world championship curtains were hung diagonally across the tables to prevent partners from signaling by gestures. As a

Have Big Club, will travel

result, the plastic bidding plaques had to be passed under the curtain. After a few days of play, an Italian pair was "accused of communicating by kicks under the table". Play was discontinued until footboards could be installed. Since that event, footboards and screens have been used in all international play and in the later rounds of major American events. Footboards notwithstanding, the Italians won again, and despite outraged protests were permitted to retain the trophy. All's fair in love, war and bridge, apparently. The stakes can be high in each. Although never definitively proven that the Blue Team cheated, from 1957 to 1975, except for the two years they didn't play, they only lost once in world competition. Since then, no Italian team has won a world championship, and the United States, using many different teams and players, has dominated the Bermuda Bowl competition. To the winners go the spoils and often the "goils".

The objectives of bridge are clearer now, so let's take a look at who and why do some people win the most. Yes, they are better players; yes they are better bidders; yes, they practice more; yes yes yes. However, the ones that win more use a better bidding system.

There's Money in The Big Club
From the card table to the hot tub

3. HISTORY OF SUCCESSFUL BRIDGE BIDDING SYSTEMS
... STANDARD AMERICAN TO PRECISION

Let me start the history lesson by quoting world renown bridge expert, Larry Cohen, on Precision or The Big Club Bidding. Larry's accolades include 26 National Championships. He was recently selected as the #23 most influential person in ACBL history. He was the 2002 ACBL Player of the Year, 2003 Sportsman of the year and 2011 Honorary member of the year. He has written many books including the best-sellers To Bid or Not to Bid and Larry teaches 2/1 Game Force. His six interactive CDs include five which were honored as "best CD of the year".

(The Big Club starts its' sexy reputation right in its' titled phallic symbol)

"Precision is a wonderful (and in my opinion, easier than "Standard") bidding systems."

All "strong" hands start with 1♣. A 1♣ opener shows approximately 16 or 17+ points.

All other 1-level openings are natural and limited (11-15).

The beauty of this system is two-fold:

1. You get to start your strong hands at the lowest possible starting point (1♣).

2. All the other 1-level openings deny very good hands, making the rest of the auction simpler.

Larry Cohen adds, "If I were teaching beginners, I would want to start them with Precision--the easiest-to-learn bidding system. As a testament to how good this system is, in my estimate, as of 2007, 4 of the top 5 pairs in America use Precision"

The magical and sexy combination of The Big Club and the weak one (1) No trump are the most important basics needed for winning bidding at bridge. Many successful teams have followed this advice and won.......big. Italians! Taiwanese! Australians! Americans! French!....."it's the bidding System Stupid", not just the player's skills and luck. The pros consistently win with Precision. There have been many earlier attempts at developing systems with these basic features ...Schenken Club, Kaplan-Sheinwold, Aces Scientific System, Alpha Opening Bids, Tangerine Club, Australian Standard Opening Bids, Bangkok Club, Blue Team Club Responses ,Kentucky Club, Breakthrough Opening Bids and Precision and many many more. However, the latest and most successful craze for the pros is the Precision Club.

The Precision Club, or Precision for short, is currently the most popular bidding system version of the strong Club and weak no trump. It was invented by the late C. C. Wei (died in 1987) assisted by Alan Truscott and first used by Taiwan teams in the late 1960's. Their success in placing second at the 1969 Bermuda Bowl launched the system's popularity.

I was prompted to write this book for two reasons.

First, I had the pleasure of playing against Kathie Wei-Sender at the PGA Regionals on June 1, 2012 in Palm Beach Gardens, Florida. Kathie and her partner were playing Precision and coincidentally, that morning, I had just read "Precision Today", the current definitive book on Precision by David Berkowitz and Brent Manley, edited and forward by Kathie Wei-Sender. As is normal, there were kibitzers watching her wonderful bidding and play. After reading the book, and being "alerted" at her table to near exhaustion by the complexities of Precision, I was convinced that Precision was not for today's average bridge player, but should be reserved for the true elites in the game, like Kathie.

(Side note, my partner and I played together for the first time and we did better than Kathie and her partner and received 4 gold points in the senior pairs the next day just showing that anyone can do well in the toughest national tournaments and competition. Since we were playing in Florida, you might expect a large number of Jewish players. Strangely, my partner, Nancy O'Donnell was Jewish and liked Irish Catholics in Boston and Kath-Wei Sender converted to Judism when she married Henry Sender when she was 60 years old.)

Second, as a recently socially eligible male, I realized that bridge tournaments have all the elements to bring together lonely potential companions. Very often people that have the time and inclination to travel to regional or national championships, alone or with a friend, are looking for more than bridge master points. The setting is perfect; away from home, at a festive hotel environment, new restaurants and bars to try, people with common interests, opportunity, easy to stop by a table and say, "how did you do on that hand that had 32 high card points?" Or better yet, I've seen you play and would love to play with you, or we could really make out well if you learned the Alterman Big Club system. What's that, you say? "You never heard of ABC!" " I'll teach you! It's based on the KISS principal." Good sexual start? Keep It Simple Stupid.

Lesson # 1: It's never too late to become a Jew, a good bridge player or find a mate later in life at the bridge table..... so read on.

It also becomes quickly apparent that complex systems like "Precision" require intimate, regular collaboration between partners, and regular practice, and discussion and communications to make partners act like a single entity at the bridge table. This immediately eliminates modern youngsters and strangers from this intimate game whose level of communications bandwidth is limited to tweets, texting and other short digital messages. This may be why the greatest game in the world, bridge, is dying. It requires collaboration in a "me only" world.

To fit in with Tweets and texting (and sexting, I might add) clearly a system of communications in Bridge is needed that is simple, focused, well sorted, and narrow band enough to enable players to learn the system independently and then come together at the bridge table or the internet without practice and collaboration and still be able to play this partnership game effectively. Welcome the Alterman Big Club. You can easily learn this simple system by yourself and nobody will ever tell you that you will go blind playing bridge with yourself.

The only thing that C.C. Wei and I have in common is that we were both trained electrical engineers. As engineers we see the beauty and difference of accuracy, precision and statistics and the core truth that communications is defined by Shannon information bandwidth and nothing else. Keep the noise and uncertainty out of the data channel. When two single people meet in a bar, the communications is very clear and focused with no ambiguity. Oh, if bridge bidding were as simple and direct as hitting on someone of the opposite sex.

After the winning of the 1964 championships once again by the Italians, Wei's curiosity prompted him to statistically analyze the notes of the Blue team given to him by Dick Frey, editor of the ACBL at the time. The Italians used artificial bidding called the Blue Team Club which grew out of the Neopolitan Club. Using statistical analysis, Wei formalized Precision which was first used by the Taiwan Chinese team in 1991 and was an attempt to make the unnatural Italian system into a more natural Precision system, initially the Taiwan Club. Ultimately readopted by the Italians, Belladonna and Garozza of the Italian team, they developed and published their Precision System where the Italians coupled a certain amount of risk taking into their game as they generally tend to do in love making and love affairs, working on the principle that the only true, everlasting love is between mother and son (Mama Mia!). The English tend to be more clinical in sex and bridge. The Americans are concerned with physical dimensions (size and strength counts, however it is equally important what you do with your god(dealt) given equipment). Americans also focus on more training of their pre-teen children in credit cards than condoms and their equivalent use of bridge gadgets like RKC to get to slams. The French are on a time table renting rooms by the hour and rushing to bridge contracts. The Japanese treat bridge and sex as transformational of spirit in an orgasm or a grand slam. When we get to the Alterman Big Club (ABC) you will note its George S. Patton simplicity combined with audacity. L'Audace, L'Audace , L'Audace.

If you ask Kathie Wei-Sender why you should play Precision, her answer is simple, "Do you want more accuracy in your bidding? Do you want to know instantly when partner fails to open 1 Club that there is no game possible on a hand? By the same token, would you enjoy the comfort of knowing, after partner opens a strong 1 club that the hand certainly belongs in game? Would you enjoy making a game forcing bid at the one level?

No matter how well you play, bidding is 75% of the game. The same is true for the "pick up" communications in a bar. Wei discovered why the Italians always won………..it was "their bidding system". However, does the average player today have the time and patience to master Precision in its details and subtleties? Also are there simplifications that improve Precision making it useable to the average player? Yes! Enter the Alterman Big Club, ABC. It's as easy as learning your ABCs and you don't need a long history of practice, discussion and play to be successful.

As in one episode of Seinfeld, where Christmas was minimized since Christianity needed history, faith, intimacy, shared experiences, planning and collaboration which made it suitable for very few of this generation, George's family practiced Festavus, an alternative holiday for the "rest of us". Festavus was easy to understand. Eat! Challenge the people around the holiday table. Competition with simple feats of strength! No subtleties. No confusion. No faith! No complexity. Festavus for the rest of us! Precision is for the elite few experts and the Alterman Big Club for the "rest of us". So how did ABC evolve? It evolved by solving many of the problems that were inherent in Precision bidding.

The central feature of the Precision system is that an opening bid of one club is used for any hand with 16 or more high card points (HCPs), regardless of distribution. An opening bid of one of a major suit signifies a five-card suit and 11-15 HCPs. A one no trump opening bid signifies a balanced hand (no five-card major suit) and 13-15 HCPs, the powerful and frightening weak opening no trump (more later on the ABC 12-15 HCP weak one (1) no trump bid).

After the success of Taiwan (Republic of China) teams in 1969 and 1970 Bermuda Bowls with the Precision system, the entire Italian Blue team switched to Precision Club and won yet another World Team Olympiad in 1972. The modifications to the system were made chiefly by Benito Garozzo and he titled it Super Precision. Today, multiple world champions Jeff Meckstroth and Eric Rodwell play their own variant known as RM Precision. (Also The Meckwell bids). Eric adds a little spice to his version of opposite sex tournament attraction by serenading the ladies with his beautiful piano playing, which I was lucky enough to observe and hear during the June 2012 PGA Regionals in Palm Beach Gardens, Florida. In North America, Precision is less commonly played than Standard American or 2/1 game forcing (expert Larry Cohen now advocates that 2/1 game force is the new Standard American), especially at the club level because of Precision's subtleties, complexities, nuances and inherent weaknesses.

Advocates of Precision say that it is generally more efficient (and precise, as the name would suggest) than systems such as Standard American because all opening bids except 1♣ are limited, the responder almost immediately knows the hand potential and the chances for a part score, game or slam.

Critics of Precision bidding, question the wisdom of combining a strong club with 5 card majors. This causes certain hand shapes to bid awkwardly, and a high percentage of hands are opened with one diamond, including in some cases hands with only a doubleton or even singleton diamond. Howard Schenken wrote in "Big Club", "This is so absurd that I wish to go on record in stating that the Big Club cannot be played with any hope of success if you attempt to use it by bidding only 5-card majors." Bob Hamman was quoted as saying, "My opinion on Precision is that combining five-card majors with a forcing club is like trying to mix oil and water, and it has serious structural defects.

Some players have even abandoned Precision in favor of a Strong Diamond System that swaps the strong 1♣ and weaker 1♦ openings. This gives the commoner weaker opening more room to bid. As we go forward, we will show that Precision is easily repaired (or just replaced) with the Alterman Big Club (ABC), a much simpler, more efficient, more precise, more natural and more fun system for the average+ player.....and it doesn't require lots of collaboration and practice.

Here is a brief summary of Precision's Main opening sequences

- **1♣**: Conventional, 16+
  - o Responses:
  - o 1♦: negative, 0-7. If playing the "impossible negative", any 4-4-4-1; this will be followed by a strong rebid.
  - o 1♥, 1♠, 2♣ 2♦: 8+, 5-card suit
  - o 1NT: 8-10, balanced
  - o 2♥, 2♠: 4-7, 6-card suit
  - o 2NT: 11-13 or 16+, balanced
  - o 3♣, 3♦, 3♥, 3♠: 4-7, 7-card suit
  - o 3NT: 14-15, balanced
- **1♦**: 11-15, no 5 card major or 6 card club suit. Sometimes a 3 card suit; some partnerships will open on a 2 card suit with shapes such as 3-3-2-5.
- **1♥, 1♠**: 11-15, 5-card suit
- **1NT**: 13-15, balanced
- **2♣**: 11-15, 6-card suit or a 5-card suit with a 4-card major
- **2♦**: Conventional (<u>Mini-Roman</u>), 11-15, 3-suited hand with singleton or void in diamond
- **2♥, 2♠**: Weak two bid, 8-10, good 6-card suit
- **2NT**: 22-24, balanced
- **3♣, 3♦, 3♥, 3♠**: normal <u>preempts</u>
- **3NT**: Conventional (<u>Gambling</u>), solid 7-card minor suit leading with AKQ, no outside strength

If you are confused already, patience, help is on the way.

Although Precision is currently the most popular weak no trump or strong club system, it was preceded by many earlier variations and system versions, the most well known being K-S (Kaplan Sheinwold), Roth-Stone and the venerable Schenken Club system

The **Kaplan-Sheinwold** (or "K-S") bidding system was developed and popularized by Edgar Kaplan and Alfred Sheinwold during their partnership, which flourished during the 1950s and 1960s. K-S is one of many **natural systems**. The system was definitively described in their 1957 book *How to Play Winning Bridge*, later reissued in paperback and still later revised.

Kaplan-Sheinwold and the Roth-Stone system were the two most influential challengers to Standard American bidding in the USA in the 1950s, 1960s, and 1970s. Although K-S is not frequently played in its original form in the 21st century, many of its features (though not the 12-14 point 1NT opening) survive in the popular 2/1 Game Forcing system. Additionally, a few elements of Kaplan-Sheinwold (notably Five-Card Majors) have become accepted as part of Standard American practice.

Among modern experts, Chip Martel and Lew Stansby play a system closely modeled on K-S, with loads of collaboration gadgets. In the late 1960s, the Precision Club system described above grafted a strong, forcing opening of 1♣ onto K-S, in effect following earlier suggestions by Marshall Miles that five-card majors and the weak no trump be added to the Schenken system. Kaplan viewed Precision with distaste, noting the disadvantages, both theoretical and at-the-table, of combining a strong club with five-card majors.

The principal features of K-S, as revised in the 1960s, are these:

1. Weak no trump. An opening bid of 1NT promises 12–14 high card points (HCP). Transfers are not used, and Stayman is non-forcing. Kaplan's highly successful partnership with Norman Kay used "Timid K-S," which departed from the original K-S structure by using a strong no trump when vulnerable.

2. Five-card majors, with limit raises. A 1NT response is forcing and responder's double is negative. 3NT is the strong, forcing raise. Two of a minor over a major suit opening is game forcing, unless rebid. 2♥ over 1♠ can be weaker (minimum is 10 points and a five card suit) than two of a minor, so as not to miss a good heart partial. Kaplan preferred to open 1♠ with 5-5 in the black suits and a minimum hand.

3. Minor suit openings are strong or unbalanced, or both, because the weak no trump handles all weak, balanced hands. A 1NT rebid by opener shows a strong no trump (15–17 HCP) and a 2NT rebid shows 18–20 HCP. Opener's reverses are forcing. Opener's simple rebids (e.g., 1 m – 1M; 2m) are restricted to absolute minimum

hands, and tend to show six cards in the minor. Opener's jump rebids (e.g., 1 m – 1M; 3m) are enormously strong, promising a hand just shy of a forcing opening bid. After a 1♦ opening, a rebid of 2♣ shows the strength and pattern of a reverse, and opener's jump to 3♣ shows a weak hand with 5-5 in the minors.

The main features of the K-S system are:

- Weak NT with conventional responses;
- Inverted Minor Raises;
- Negative Double;
- 5-Card Majors with 1NT Forcing response;
- Limit Jump Raises;
- Weak Two Bids;
- Strong 2♣;
- 3NT opening shows a 2NT hand (20-22 points) with a solid long minor suit
- Cue Bids;
- Gerber;
- Blackwood;
- Grand Slam Force;
- Roman Asking Bids;
- Takeout Doubles;
- Weak Jump Overcalls;

Another early strong 1♣ system was the Schenken Club system.

The main features of the Schenken Club system are:

- 1♣ is bid on hands of 17+ points, or 14+ hands that are strongly distributional;
- 1♦ is the negative response showing 0-6 points. 2♣ is a semi-positive response showing 7-8 points, including at least one ace or king, and promises a rebid. Any other response is forcing to game; Other 1 bids are limited, and responder normally passes with less than 8 points;
- Strong NT; 17-19 HCP

- 2♣ is natural and shows at least a five card suit. 2♦ asks for a 4 card major;
- 2♦ opening asks about honors. 2♥ denies an ace, other minimum responses are ace-showing, except 2NT, which show the A♥ With 2 aces, responder jumps in the higher ranking suit with touching suits, 3NT with non-touching aces, or 4♣ with the black aces. Opener can respond in the cheapest suit to ask for kings. A 2NT rebid over 2♥ shows 23-25 points, and 3NT shows 26-27;
- 2♥ and 2♠ are <u>Weak Two Bids</u>;
- 2NT shows at least 5-5 in the minors;
- <u>Gambling 3NT</u>;
- 3♣ shows a solid 6 or seven card suit with 10-15 points.

Why did the Schenken Club bidding system disappear??

It was not natural, unclear and not very precise.

How do we take the best from all these systems, simplify it, eliminate the problems, not require practice and collaboration, strengthen responses, leverage off interfering bids to help us, not hurt us!

From Standard American (including 2 over 1) to modern Precision we see great complexity of bids and responses leaving ambiguities and uncertainties. Often the wrong player is the declarer in no trump contracts. Interference bids disrupt Precision players. Not enough focus on disruption of opponents reaching low level, makeable contracts. Bidding gets to high levels before partners realize they don't have a game or slam. ABC adds KISS to biding. ABC leverages off interferers bids. ABC weak no trump is disruptive to opponents, adding a fog of war over the auction. ABC allows the partners to easily select who will be no trump declarer. ABC tells partnership at level one bids the potentials for game, slam or devastating penalties to interfering bidders……………….. And it is as easy to learn as ABC. ABC can be used as presented in the next chapter or grafted on to your favorite bids. You chose. Try it. You will like it. No, you will love it!

4. ALTERMAN BIG CLUB SYSTEM
... SIMPLE AS ABC (STRONG ONE CLUB/WEAK ONE NO TRUMP) FOR THE REST OF US.

The ABC Opening 1 Club bid: I'll show you mine quickly and then you can show me yours slowly.

4.1 A Big Club opening bid of 1 Club promises 16 or more high card points but at least 15 plus distributional points. Total points include high card points (HCP) and distributional points (points are derived from Standard American). There is NO other strong bid. (Two no trump or Three no trump may or may not be used and could be used for a special personalized bid but is not part of ABC) One club REQUIRES a response from partner to show his Aces & Kings and also high card point (HCP) count using a major innovation of ABC, controls/steps. (we'll talk about interfering bids later) (only aces or kings are counted(controls) or all HCPs may be counted(steps) or a combination of both, depending on your preference)

You showed me your Big Club, now I'll show you my body parts

4.2 Responder to the Big Club opener is REQUIRED to bid step responses and bids 1 diamond with a maximum of one King (simple version....0-3 HCP points), 1 heart with one Ace or two kings (simple version...4-6 HCP). 1 spade with one ace and one king, two aces or 3 kings (simple version.....7-9 HCP), there are two steps that show 10-12 HCP. 1NT shows a balanced 10-12 HCP and no problem with opening lead coming around to responder at ultimate NT contract. This is a critical advantage

Worth a Big Club Bid!

of ABC vs. Precision. Very often Precision bidding yields the wrong player as no trump declarer. That is not true in ABC, where responder to big club opener decides who will be the NT declarer depending upon the shape of his hand. 2 Clubs shows generally unbalanced hand with 10-12 HCP. 2 diamonds shows 13-15 HCP, 2 hearts shows16-18 HCP, 2 spades shows19-21 HCP and 2 NT with 22-23 HCP (very seldom do these last two responses occur over an opening hand that has 16 or more points). All these step response bids are artificial and must be alerted.

Interference over Big Club...Opponents can try to interfere with good communications between partners....but wind up inadvertently helping them.

4.3 If an opponent after 1 Club opener is brave enough to jump in with an interfering bid(over a hand that promises 16 or more HCP....actually as much as 37 HCP.... and hasn't told his suit or distribution yet before responder makes his HCP step or controls/steps, God bless him since he is in for a surprise. With interference, responder now changes his step controls/HCP responses as follow. Pass (alertable) is at most one king (simple version....0-3 HCP points), double is one ace or two kings(simple version...4-6 HCP), one suit higher than interferer is one ace and one king, two aces, or three kings (simple version.....7-9 HCP), two suits higher is 10-12 points etc. Again, 1NT or 2C (or 2NT or 3C) show the same number of HCP with distribution differences as above. Let's focus on the "double bid" response meaning One Ace or two Kings (simple version...4-6 HCP), a critical bid that should make any opponent interferer nervous. If interferer doubles ABC 1 Club opening bid, added steps are available to responder. Pass is 0-3 HCP, redouble is 4-6 HCP, 1 diamond is 7-9 HCP etc.(or controls if you chose that option)

When an interferer jumps into the middle of a Big Club solicitation and partners responses, the interferer becomes part of a threesome of players enhancing the performance of the response sequence to a ménage a trios sequence, thus aiding the ABC bidders.

If the 1 club opener has a minimum bid, say 16-18 points and his partner has only one ace or two kings (simple version…4-6 HCP), it is unlikely that they have game and are now in the position to leave the doubled interfering bid in with about 20-24 defense points, drooling at their prospects for big penalties, if they chose. Bidding 1 higher than interferer responder promises at least one ace and one king, two aces, or three kings (simple version…..7-9 HCP), and a likely game try or better.

You saw my Big Club baby, now learn about the rest of what I got!

4.4 The 1 club opener's next bid is his suit or NT. If he bids 1 NT he has 16-18 HCP and a balanced hand with no 5 card majors, 2 NT shows 19-21 HCP and a balanced hand with no 5 card majors, 3NT more than 22 HCP and balanced, 2 of any suit shows at least five cards and a minimum 1 club opener(16-18 points). With a minimum rebid by 1 club opener, responder may pass with only one Ace or two Kings and no other biddable suit of his own. If responder has shown a minimum of one Ace and one King, two Aces or three Kings he could pass with 7 points and must bid with 9 points after opening 1 club bidders second bid of a suit. If 1 club openers second bid is NT, responder may use Stayman, Smolen or transfers. Any jump bid of a suit by opening 1 club bidder is forcing. If responder showed one ace or two kings (simple version…4-6 HCP), opening 1 club bidder may bid 2 NT showing 19-21 points indicating an interest in 3 NT or is open to Stayman or transfers. All these bids are very natural and point count/control oriented. Opening 1C then rebid jump to 3 NT shows 22+ HCP (Stayman & transfers in)

Bid slowly, ABC is like making love…….don't jump your partner because you have a hot hand…slowly is better

4.5 RKC(Blackwood) (14-30) for Majors and (30-14) for minors, DEPO and Gerber are all available after the texture and point counts are known.

4.6 Opening one club bidders next bid is a function of responders step response point count and is all natural. Any jump bid is

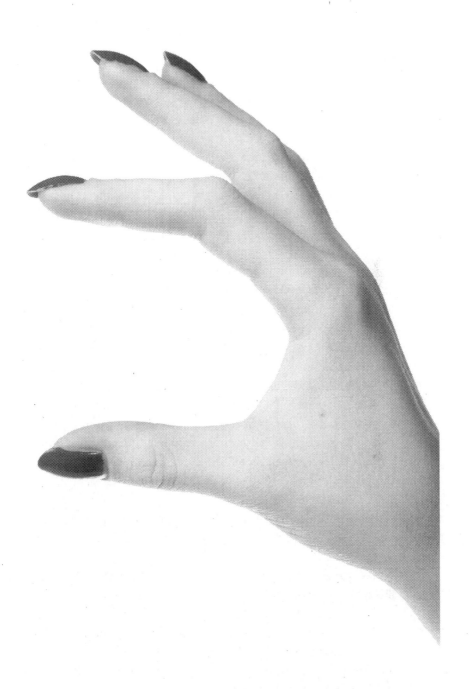

Size Matter in Bridge Bids and Sex.

game forcing and may be invitational to slam depending on the responders point count. All natural.

When opening bidder doesn't have a 1 club opener, the benefits of the ABC system are even more important. When you can't whip out your Big Club, partnerships can still be fun, sexy and easy

4.7 Opening bids of 1 of a major are limit bids of 11-15 points with 5 or more of the major. Responder may pass with 8 or fewer points, (waiting in the bushes for future developments) support the major at the 2 level with 9-11 points or bid 4 of the major with good support and 12-14 points. 2 NT shows 12-14 points and no bid major support. 3 NT show 16-18 HCP and is invitational to slam if opener had 14-15 points. Very natural. New suit is forcing and jump shift by responder forcing to game and invitational. Responder jumps in major to 3 is very weak with at least 4 of major. There is no Jacoby transfer over an opening 1 of a major. With 4 of the major and an opening hand, responder bids 4 of the major directly since the maximum of opener Is 15 points plus 12-14 by responder is below slam level interest. With 16 or more points, responder may invite to slam with a jump shift (forcing to game) but a minimum rebid by opener will discourage slam and go to game (3 NT with only 5 card major or to 4 of the major with 6 or more. Any other bid shows a maximum opener and slam interest.

How to screw your opponents coyly while being naked for your partner. Submissive /weak 1 No Trump

4.8 The very important (adds fog to the battlefield) but weak opening bid of 1 NT shows 12-15 HCP (Stayman and transfers are in) no five card majors (maybe a weak 5 card heart suit) but MAY have worthless doubletons or a singleton (singleton Ace or King restriction at The Bridge Place only, local rule) or 5 diamonds or 5 clubs. With five clubs, a 2 club opening may be bid and with 5 diamonds, 1 diamond may be bid if bidder can't meet opening 1 NT requirements (no worse than singleton Ace or King at The Bridge Place). Over weak (12-15 HCP)1 NT openers, 3c is long clubs and invitational, 3 d is long diamonds and invitational, 3H is 5X5 in majors but non forcing (10-12) and 3 Spades is 5X5 in majors and forcing (13 + points). Smolen works too.

What can opponents do vs. the ABC devastating weak one no trump. They try anything and everything but it doesn't work well. Hamiliton/ Cappeletti, Meckwell..............What's Meckwell? We will get to that next chapter.

Now for the dreaded, one (1) diamond or two club opener.

One diamond is like an engagement ring, avoid them if you can. Beware, like an artificial engagement stone, it can be full of lies (ie only one diamond,) inviting unknowing partner into a faulty, unreasonable interaction with a potential disastrous contract

4.9 ABC Opening bid of 1 diamond shows 12-15 HCP and no 5 card major and could be short and as few 1 diamond (must be alerted!). This only occurs if bidder cannot open one no trump due to some local club requirements of a minimum of a singleton king or ace. Remember that the phrase "could be short" in an ABC 1 diamond opening carries less negative connotation than in sex! (With 12-15 points, opener will bid 1 NT if he meets requirement rather than open with 1 diamond).

The ugly two (2) club opening bid......like two men looking for a ménage a trios..... raunchy & weak, looking for a strong partner to find an exciting experience that can also be fun.

4.10. Opening bid of 2 clubs shows 12-15 total points and at least a 5 card club suit and no 5 card majors and either a void or useless singleton(local Bridge Place club restrictions, not ACBL) and couldn't open 1 NT originally.

4.11. Miscellaneous bids: Weak two bids (except 2 clubs) are 6-10 points and OGUST responses over 2NT forcing (or key cards if you are afraid of OGUST). Weak 3 bids are standard.

Over opponents 1 NT opening, I prefer 2C shows both minors, 2D show both majors and 2 s and 2H are 6 card natural bids and double is 15-17, but ABC allows whatever system you chose, Hamilton, Cappeletti , Dont . Meckwell etc

It is important to note the ABC quantifies NT bids exactly at 12-15, 16-18, 19-21, 22+ and allows Stayman, Smolen and transfers at each of these bids.

The ABC system does not use opening 2 No Trump or 3 No Trump bids as other bidding systems often use. You and your partner may chose to use these bids for particular hands if you like or not use them at all. For example, you might decide to use an opening 2 No Trump bid to show 25-27 HCP rather than open 1 Club and then jump to 3 No Trump.

Is that all? No more? You're kidding?.....What about.........and .....and..... nothing! You "loined" (pardon the sexual innuendo) the ABC system!

5. A DIGRESSION

... HOW DO OPPONENTS TRY TO DEFEND AGAINST THE WEAK ONE NO TRUMP OPENING BID? MECKWELL? OTHER?

ABC has two primary features, the only strong opening bid is 1 Club (over 16 High Card points-HCP) and the weak one no trump opening bid of 12-15 HCP. In the last chapter we showed that normal interference (Fog of War) bids made by opponents against other artificial strong club openers are thwarted by ABC, actually using the interferers bid to our own advantage in conveying information and even penalizing the interferer for making such bids. In this chapter we will illustrate that our own introduction of a Fog Of War to opponents bidding using the ABC weak one no trump opening bid as often as possible adds complexity and difficulty to the opponents. Using the typical strong one no trump opener of 15-18 HCP, the chances that a game can be made by the opponents is small since the most combined strength they can possess is about 22-25 HCP, normally inadequate for game. Using a weak one no trump, the opponents can have 25-28 combined HCP and have a natural game, if they can find it or a majority of the strength for a part score, again if they can find it without going too high and getting doubled. So, in this chapter we digress to what opponents do to eliminate the fog of was of weak one no trumps, as well as normal one no trump bids. As a minor digression, let me address the lengths players will go to design bids after one no trump is opened by the opponents. Hamiliton/Cappeletti, DONT, Meckwell ? Yes, I'm talking about all the above, but let me go into Meckwell in more depth. Most good players don't have any idea of what Meckwell is and the average club player is overwhelmed with the complexity and degree of planning, practice and playing together that Meckwell requires. That certainly is not our goal in ABC since Meckwell would be the equivalent of 5 hours of foreplay and then making a move on your partner after they are asleep.

The foundation of the Meckwell convention is really employed only against a *strong No Trump opening bid* with a minimum of 14 high card points. An exclusion of the Meckwell defense method is not apparent to the average bridge player for weaker No Trump opening bids, such as those with values ranging from 10 to 13 points. However both Mr. Jeff Meckstroth and Mr. Eric Rodwell employ a different set of guidelines for a defense method against a *weak No Trump opening bid*, with a start between 10 and 13 high card points. This defense method is also shown below to emphasize the difficulty of dealing with 12-15 point weak no trump opening bids as we use often in ABC.

The state of vulnerability does not influence the employment of the Meckwell conventional defense method.

Guidelines of the Meckwell Defense Method Against an Opposing 1 No Trump with 14 plus Points

Double: Shows either a single Minor suit or both Major suits. The advancer bids 2♣, which is a completely artificial bid. The intervenor corrects to 2 Diamonds if Diamonds is the Minor suit, or bids one of the Major suits to show both Major suits.

Intervenor Continuations

Pass: If the responder of the No Trump bidder bids, then the advancer has the option to pass when holding few values. The intervenor can continue to compete.

2 ♦: Shows the single-suited holding with Diamonds.

2 ♥: Shows both Major suits. Both suits are of or about the same value and length. The advancer corrects to Spades only if support for Spades is stronger.

2 ♠: Shows both Major suits. However, by bidding Spades first, then the Spades are stronger in *working values* as compared to Hearts, the second suit.

3 ♣: If the single-suited holding is indeed Clubs, then the intervenor raises the level of bidding to the third level. Since the intervenor knows that the advancer must respond 2♣, then the Club holding should contain about 3 winning tricks and *working values* such as AKQxx or AKJ10xx. This is owing to the fact that the advancer may hold a shortage in Clubs.

2 ♣:   Promises Clubs and and a Major suit.
2 ♦:   Promises Diamonds and a Major suit.
2 ♥:   Natural bid in Hearts. The accepted length is 5 cards with about 3 winning tricks, else a 6-card plus length.
2 ♠:   Natural bid in Spades. The accepted length is 5 cards with about 3 winning tricks, else a 6-card plus length.
2 NT: Promises both Minor suits.

Example of the Meckwell Defense Method

East	South
♠ A985	♠ KQ763
♥ K106	♥ AQ974
♦ QJ10	♦ K7
♣ AK5	♣ 6

East	South	West	North	Meaning
1 NT				The range is established as between 14-18 points.
	Double			The Meckwell defense method showing either a single-suited holding in one of the Minor suits, or a holding with both Major suits.
		Pass		The responder has no bid.
			2 ♣	The advancer is forced to bid 2 Clubs in order for the intervenor to clarify the holding.

Pass	A logical pass in order to defend. If the responder has passed following the double, then the responder holds insufficient values and length to compete.
2 ♥	Shows both Major suits. Both suits are of or about the same value and length. The advancer corrects to Spades only if support for Spades is stronger.
2 ♠	This would be the less preferable rebid to show both Major suits in this particular example since they are of about the same length and strength. By bidding Spades first, then the promise is that the Spade suit is stronger in *working values* as compared to Hearts, the second suit.

Note: With the above auction the bid of 2 Hearts would be the more accurate bid. Although the Heart suit contains 1.5 winning tricks as opposed to the Spade suit holding only 1 winning trick, the length is the same. The logic is that since both Major suits are of equal length it is preferable to bid Hearts first in order to provide the advancer with a preference, which could occur on the two level. By showing both Major suits with a first rebid of 2 Spades, then the partnership is forced to the three level if the advancer holds better and longer Hearts.

Guidelines of the Meckwell (sort of) Defense Method Against an Opposing Weak 1 No Trump with 10-13 Points (12-15 points in ABC)

Although this defense method is not officially designated as Meckwell against Weak No Trump, this is the essence of the following defense method, which originated with Mr. Jeff Meckstroth and Mr. Eric Rodwell. Talk about complex systems.

Following a 10-13 point or 12-15 HCP used in ABC 1 No Trump opening by an opponent then the guidelines ala Meckwell for competing become different as opposed to the opening bid of a stronger No Trump. Oy Veh! Can Meckstroth or Rodwell be Jewish? You could never learn Hebrew and Meckwell simultaneously.

Double: The *double* is unique in that it shows also a holding, which matches or strongly compares with the No Trump holding of the opponent and contains the same range of values.

East	South
♠ A985	♠ QJ10
♥ K106	♥ A985
♦ QJ10	♦ K97
♣ K105	♣ QJ8

2 ♣: Promises Spades and a *rounded suit*, either Hearts or Clubs

2 ♦: Promises Diamonds and an unspecified Major suit.

2 ♥: Promises a single-suited holding in Hearts, natural. The length is either a 5-card suit with 3 winning tricks, or else a 6-card plus suit.

2 ♠: Promises a single-suited holding in Spades, natural. The length is either a 5-card suit with 3 winning tricks, or else a 6-card plus suit.

2 NT: Shows a single-suited holding in a Minor suit. The advancer relays to Clubs.

Do you see what I mean? This Meckwell stuff takes collaboration, practice and I'm still not sure that it makes any sense. Unlike sex, nobody really expects you to play bridge with the same partner for the rest of your life and have the time and energy to learn all their moves, as Meckwell requires.

6. REVIEW OF ABC VS. PRECISION
... WHAT HAVE YOU LEARNED?

The goal of The Alterman Big Club is to develop a simple system that bridge players can learn on their own, separately, and come to the bridge table with little or no discussion, practice or collaboration and successfully bid attaining above average results with any other partner who plays ABC, much like sex. What a great way to make new friends and lovers as well for that matter. We invoke the KISS (Keep it simple stupid) principle to allow players to learn ABC as easy as they did their ABCs. We believe that "Better is the enemy of good enough", a famous saying. No need for a variety of bids (or moves) to show a strong hand (hit on); one Big Club is enough. Jacoby 2 NT, 2 over 1, one no trump forcing, waiting bids etc. are just artefacts to try to straighten out a poor bidding system, Standard American, and/or a poor seduction plan. Get it right in the first place with The Big Club. Ambiguity at the bridge table is as bad as ambiguity between lovers. ABC is straight talk between bridge lovers, lovers of bridge and lovers of loving. Like good sex, don't be upset by a few initial failures. Comparable with sex, don't give up ABC even if your partner loses temporary interest in it.

ABC is the most precise system ever developed. 3 point precision is obtained, not more. It is important to note the ABC quantifies NT bids exactly at 12-15, 16-18, 19-21, 22+ and allows Stayman, Smolen and transfers at each of these bids.

Like the three point landing of an airplane, ABC describes your hands perfectly and inserts your big Club into partners proper openings. If you have a shapely fit with your partner, don't be embarrassed to say so and show him/her. ABC does this with natural, simple bidding rules and none of the complexity and ambiguities of Precision. ABC is Precise. Precision is imprecise.

In our cyber world of modern communications, hackers are always trying to disrupt, destroy and steal what doesn't belong to them. In bridge we call these opponent villains, interfering bidders. Most bidding systems, in particular artificial bidding systems like Precision or the normal Big Club systems, are susceptible to these interfering villains scullduggery. In ABC, like Tai Kwon Do or Ju Jitsu , we use the villains bid with his leverage to enhance our communications in the presence of these interfering bids, and not be a victim of them. On the other hand, we frequently use the most disruptive cyber attack bid of all time, the ultimate fog of war generator, the weak one no trump, to throw opponents off balance. They really don't handle well our demure and coy 12-15 point opening one no trump bids which we do as often as possible in ABC. Even the Meckwell boys don't like it.

Speaking of no trump, precision bidding is a victim of itself in that very often the wrong partner is inadvertently playing the no trump contract. No control! Uncontrolled responses can be the same problem in love making and other interactions. Unlike sex, "fast arrival" has no negative connotation.

ABC enables no trump control by giving the players absolute choice as to who is the no trump declarer. Who is on top, in other words.

As simple as ABC is, it leaves much room to personalize between partners a variety of favorite bids, not absolutely necessary for success, but introduced to give the collaborating partner a small edge. It's much like lovers who don't have to talk to each other to communicate what they mean or feel. Like the Cialis add says; those cute little things she does that excite you. If an added bid "turns you on" go ahead and do it. It won't hurt ABC and is not necessary for playing success but it does put a little spice in your game and partnership. KISS and adding personal "hot spots" adds some sex to an intellectual pursuit. Teaching and playing ABC is sexy. Have fun. Let Your Big Club loose and it will pay handsome dividends. Think of ABC as adding Viagra to your repertoire. You may not always need it but it could come in handy in a pinch (or a clinch).

I Hate That Big Club Weak No Trump

I overheard this discussion at the last PGA regional tournament. With an unsuccessful and lonely tournament apparent result, a lady said to her partner, apologetically, with the bridge director standing nearby, "I guess all those f----ing lessons I took over the winter didn't help."The bridge director immediately responded, "Well, there you have it. You should have taken ABC bridge lessons instead!" (An old joke but very appropriate).You can buy the ABC book on IUniverse.com, Amazon. com, Barnes & Noble.com and maybe your local market.

Finally, I would like to make a disclaimer. Some of you that attempt to follow my recommendations, not on bridge, but on increasing your social sexual life, may have to develop more guts or chutspa to succeed. As a Doctor (I confess again, Dr. of engineering), there is a medical distinction. We've all heard about people having Guts or Chutspa, but do you really know the medical difference between them? In an effort to keep you fully informed, here are the definitions:

GUTS - Is arriving home late after a extra late night playing bridge, being met by your wife or intimate friend with a broom, and having the **Guts** to ask: 'Are you still cleaning, or are you flying somewhere?'

Chutspa - Is coming home late after a night out ostensibly playing bridge, smelling of perfume and beer, lipstick on your collar, slapping your wife or intimate friend on the ass and having the **chutspa** to say: 'You're next, Chubby.'

I hope this clears up any confusion on the definitions. Medically, speaking there is no difference in the outcome. Both result in sudden death. Enjoy all the benefits of ABC bridge and stay alive and healthy and remember that bridge can lead to other exciting things besides becoming a life master.

Normal Bridge has proved that you can sit for hours in front of somebody without once making eye contact. Let's try to change that. Who knows? You might even meet the partner of your dreams playing the Alterman Big Club.

Let's Play Big Club Tonight

Printed in the United States
By Bookmasters